LIFE ON VENUS

DOMINIQUE WRITES

LIFE ON VENUS

DOMINIQUE WRITES

Illustrations by: Esmaes.art

Pre-Production by: Nadine King

DominiqueWrites.com

"I write because my emotions build and become intense

you'll need a little time and some thought to digest

My spirit is acute to everything I hear and see

I write because it's the only spacewhere my mind can breathe."

Dominique Writes

CONTENTS

PART THREE – then comes growth   **51**

For the loves that taught me
along the way.

PART ONE:

In the beginning

HER

I often contemplate the space I'm in
and allow my mind to fly
It soars through my subconscious
and my imagination runs wild.
I replay moments passed and try to
perfect what should have been
conversations I would have had
if I could relive the scene.
I focus too hard on my future self
and how I want to progress
haunted by the past and certain
experiences I'd rather forget.
I consciously overthink things
and then they play on my mind
Writing it down has a way of helping me
accept them over time.

Opinionated as I am, no doubt my
arguments are seamless
though when articulated in voice
I often end up speechless.
I'm an emotional reactor and my heart
activates before my brain
but a logical way of thinking, when I
keep my feelings contained.
If you delve into my mind, you'll find
the paradise of a hoarder
as I obsess over details until I can
find some sort of order.
The way things tumble out sometimes is
down to trial and error
But given a pen and some paper
my world becomes much clearer.

The hailstones came down and on my skin
I felt the pain
I heard the roaring thunder and I saw
the thick rain
Salty rivers overflowing clouding up my
brain
Muddy footprints over flesh can leave a
stain.

Nothing could be done because there's no
sun to intervene
Bullet proofed up but inside the waves
scream
Cold and bare but deep down I
still believe
In merrily and merrily coz life is but a
dream.

Then after winter optimism breeds and
spring is born
Everything gets brighter and the ice
starts to thaw
But slowly never quick to reveal the red
core
For fear that one day the cold could
respawn.

So the shadows still remain but the sun
rays like to flirt
Giving hope that one day the dark skies
will disperse
In time trees blossom and the bark no
longer hurts
My palette is dry and only warmth can
quench my thirst.

In struts Summertime with a golden
embracing smile
Nurturing the spirit like a mother to
a child
All is forgotten... if only for a while
for the sale-by date looms as happiness
is on trial.

But until judgement day comes we gladly
cherish the bliss
Laughter is abundant and the frowns are
never missed
It's all a distant memory as if it
ceased to exist
Innocence is restored and the Fall is
just a myth.

THE ELEPHANT

Left to loiter around the edges
Detesting this placement
But encouraged to embrace it

Nothing but an innocent child
In the wrong by default
But was it the elephant's fault?

THE WOLF AND THE SHEEP

The Black Sheep stood naked with her
innocence stripped away
The words she had been groomed with were
tattooed on her skin.

His name had been banished from memory a
long time ago
but his presence had lingered, leaving a bad
taste in her mouth.

He extended himself as kin and so they
were blind to the sin
that over time he had indulged and
tainted her with.

So brazen with his displays and
eccentric in his ways,
they didn't see his faults and would
refuse to believe had they
been told.

He penetrated her mind with thoughts
that drained away her purity.
She developed a mental maturity more
advanced than her body understood.

He had primed her too early and at times
she felt dirty so turned to boys who
offered her comforting smiles and open
arms.

They were simply taking advantage of what he
had started but she went along, assuming
sincerity on their part.

She gave in to their charms as they took turns
leaving invisible scars
and she'd go back for more, until the wounds
ached, and they remained raw.

Silence would be her demise, but she refused
to confide, instead, learned to look into eyes
whilst telling white lies.

She knew she shouldn't have done nothing, and
she would have said something
but Sheep have been trained not to cry Wolf.

SMELL THE ROSES

She dreamt of pretty things
being best friends, holding hands and
making plans of what to bake.
Life in her head always smelt of roses and
mother's carrot cake
In reality roses wilt, falling to the ground.
Her smile was fake.

Please don't interrupt me whilst I'm
sitting in my darkest place
the smile has gone and there's no trace
my mood is not permitting me to go and
find my happy face
wallowing in all those pessimistic
things that I've got stowed
and now I'm out about to blow
about one hundred and one things that
you don't even know but you *will* know
that I've been depressed about this
stressing 'bout this and now I'm getting
vex about it
don't tell me there isn't sense to this
as I'm feeling extra sensitive
bomb exploding in three, two- why did
you even mention it?
we've been through this so many times
before
all you had to do was just ignore
but then you opened the door and now
there's more to come
I'm not even close to being done about
nothing in particular but everything at
once.

STRANDED

Shipwrecked
on a lonely island
once trodden on
now forgotten
cast away
communication forbidden

I have a little box underneath my breast
where ugly things are kept.
They get pushed down so far over time
that I'm not sure of its depth,
but every once in a while I feel a
tightening in my chest
and it's a warning sign for me to find a
private place for them to eject.

I get a knot in the back of my throat
when those ugly things start to rise.
They keep coming up one by one and form
themselves into a cry,
the tears gush out and my spirit slowly
drowns in monstrous sounds,
I allow myself to lose control and in
self-pity I wallow.

I'm bleeding on the inside from those
ugly things that I hide.
But you want to see her pretty, and you
want to see her smile,
so I stare at my reflection as I regain
my strength and pride,
I'm a woman after all and sometimes that's
the biggest fight.

Ugly things can happen to beautiful
people.
It doesn't mind nor matter if she wants
it or not.
They're forced upon you whilst your will
is restrained
and they choose not to hear when you
silently scream stop.

I was sitting here thinking, wondering
about life
and all that comes with it, be it
happiness or strife.
The cards that are dealt when you come
to rise
the moves that you play until you close
your eyes.

Because, I associate this world with a
game.
You take your move and then patiently wait
to see what strike the other will make,
whilst you strategically plan your own
fate.

I keep it hidden, keep my direction
concealed
until the instant it needs to be
revealed
then I take my turn and all is fulfilled
and for a short time, life is bliss and
surreal.

When you play your cards right,
things turn out good.
Everything connects in the ways that
they should

your position is known and completely
understood
you occasionally look back at where you
once stood.

And then, that moment again when a hand
is played
the panic sets in and your confidence
strays.
Prepare for battle and engage the poker
face
Do you throw in the towel or do you keep
the faith?

Up to the day you're confronted by
exposure
heavily wounded and your reactions are
slower.
The end of the game is constantly
drawing closer
Until the screen reads 'Game Over'.
Life's over.

Explain it, but don't
tell me your feelings.

You say... I don't
care to understand it really.

MY HEART BEATS

Sometimes my heart beats with such a
vengeance that it must be in love.
I feel it pump so hard ready to elope
away from its sanctuary beneath my
bosom.

Sometimes my heart beats with such a
rhythm that it must be feeling passion.
It starts off slow but gets
progressively faster until it reaches
its climax and flutters.

Sometimes my heart burns and the pain
keeps me awake all night.
It hurts so bad that I struggle
to inhale and there are times it pierces my
skin.

Sometimes my heart skips a beat and I
wait anxiously for it to be ignited.
I have to shock it into action and I
worry that one day its stubbornness
will take over.

Sometimes my heart beats so steadily
that it's barely making any effort at
all.
These are the times I'm most uneasy as I
know it's waiting for the right time to
end.

Sometimes my heart beats for me but I
wish it could beat for others.
I'd never need the words to explain
exactly how I feel because they'd be
feeling it too.

HEAD versus HEART

A mother's love without her child
is that of eternal longing
like a shadow skulking around
searching for a sense of belonging
What was once growing there
brought feelings of nervous joy
now all has purposely disappeared
and lives have been destroyed

She liked to love and loved to laugh as
deep as the earth's core
Her passion was fierce and her soul was
raw though shunned by the ones she
yearned for.
Emotionally acute she felt their words
as one by one they battered
her smile faded and her spirit burned,
she was forgotten and her ashes
scattered.
Broken down and isolated she succumbed
grudgingly to her woes
"they won't know what they've got till
it's gone"
she thought, as the old saying goes.
She looked out into the world and
watched as the mist rose,
then took her last breath and relaxed as
her heart froze.

DÉJÀ VU

Cheap perfume
old cigarettes
sweet alcohol
You smell
like the mother you ran from
in a desperate plea
not to be
the woman she had become.

Cheap
old
sickly sweet
He looks
like the man she hid you from
in a desperate plea
for you not to meet
the stranger she had learned to love.

LOST MIND

Emptiness has trapped her in a state of
depression.
She doesn't enjoy life but she'll fake a
smile to avoid questions.
Foggy are her thoughts and blank are her
expressions.
Her mind wanders through the haze, the
path removed in all directions.

Helpful hands around her neck restrict
her determination.
Her appeals aren't heard and she gets
lost in translation.
Words tumble out in the wrong order and
there's no penetration
to the ear that wants to care but fails
to understand her motivations.

She blocks out the unknowing mouths who
try to referee.
Their voices are muddled.
It's unbearable. She can't breathe.
It's a struggle to break away from the
dictatorship she perceives.
Her fight to be free is misunderstood so
her heart continues to bleed.

PART TWO:

lessons are learned

FALLING THROUGH IT ALL

I'm here through thick and thin,
by your side through it all
I'll dance to the beat with you and
catch you if you fall
I'm here through your woes but have my
own, thrown at me by all
So if I'm absent from your day,
know that I may be about to fall.

I never met you but emotions backed up
in my throat when you died.
Hearing the words they used to describe
you made me upset that we were
strangers.
You were taken prematurely before our
connection could aspire beyond passing
ships,
so I mourned the warm smile that I could
only imagine seeing.
There was a familiarity in the remnants
of your energy that engulfed us all.
It soothed everyone's grief and for a
moment we melted the gloom,
Our voices came together as the opening
chords chimed for the first hymn. But
"gone too soon" were the only words
that we could manage to sing.

ROLLERCOASTER

I think you like it when I cry
when the river overflows to make
waterfalls running down the face of
heartbreak.
You make my heart ache.
Let's get off this merry go round
I'm feeling dizzy now with angry words
weaving through my cloudy throbbing
mind.
You're no longer mine.
Let's hold hands and take a leap
fast forward to the promised future when
the high has returned steadily rising
again.
You're my best friend.
Staring doey eyed into each other's eyes
magical sparks reignite those fluttering tummy
flies and our limbs are
interlaced.
I claimed your name.

I quietly enjoyed every second you were mine
Did you feel my love transfer through to
your lifeline?
I had visions of who you might look
like. His eyes, my smile.
I just wanted to hold you if only for a
while.

I was thrilled with my little secret but
I knew I couldn't keep it.
I just needed to believe it even though
we hadn't conceived it.
Still, I prayed over you and embraced
the sickness you gave me.
I was glowing knowing that your presence had
saved me.

I quietly enjoyed every second you were mine
But it all flat lined with that dreaded single line
I ignored the pain when it came and brushed it off as other things
For sure I felt the signs of life that confirmed your being.

I drowned in the red sea as it washed away my truth
I wanted what I was due and I tried to ignore the proof
I wanted to cling on to those feelings you gave me but I had to let go,
so R.I.P to the woman you made me.

Today I woke up feeling empty.

Empty like the stove in a poor person's
kitchen
Empty like a homeless man without a pot
to piss in
Empty like the body whose soul has left
it for dead
Empty like my stomach battling feelings
of dread

Empty like a heart struggling to catch
the last beat
Empty like the shoes walking a mile with
no feet
Empty like the small talk with someone
you don't know
Empty like the candle whose flame has
been blown

Empty like a library stripped of all its
books
Empty like a jar remaining silent when
shook
Empty like this cycle of life we're
living in
Empty like the smile she's perfected
giving

Empty like the womb which just
miscarried a baby
Empty like the promises that were
downgraded to maybes
Empty like the sleeps which ran out of
nightmares
Empty like my eyes which are drained of
every tear

IT'S NOT ME, IT'S HER

I should be happy for you
that's what my minds says
But my heart is complaining it should be
me instead
And though the smile on my face is
somewhat genuine
a battle of emotion is taking place in
my head

You didn't want mine and you were so
adamant
Now a few months in
she's carrying our blessing
Would things be different if I had
pushed for it?
I'd be the one on the pedestal and not
just time spent

Whilst I didn't want to force you into
anything
I have this niggling feeling it should
be me winning
Morally I don't believe in entrapment
But it turns out I'm the one lonely in
the end

I wonder if you feel the same,
do we share the regret?
Something's telling me that you're not
over it yet
A million thoughts of things I should
have done and said
But on the outside I remained speechless

SECRET RITUALS

She waited in silence for his weekly
release
Counted cracks in the walls until he was
pleased.
Sometimes she lay still, face down in
the sheets
Just to ensure their eyes wouldn't meet.

Long ago she had perfected the art of
faking
Not that he cared for the sounds she was
making.
She used to think sleep was a means of
escaping
Then realised his morals she had
mistaken.

Motionless she stayed until he was
finished
Covered her body as her self-respect
diminished
His intoxication had made this by far
the quickest
And for that she was grateful as it only
took minutes.

As per usual she would leave him passed
out for an hour
Her expression was stone cold in the
piping hot shower
She prayed continuously for this month's
red flower
if that didn't come the consequence
would be dire.

Dead eyes conceal the window to your
soul
blinding me from your thoughts and
feelings
blocking me from the inside with fake
smiles
outwardly fronting. I'm searching for
the spark once so appealing.
Shrinking down trying to make yourself
disappear
you shy away when I enter your presence
and as I desperately claw at what we had
before,
your spirit runs from me increasing its
distance.

Dead eyes grudgingly greet me when I
come home.
Your gaze struggles, not wanting to meet
mine
happy as I am to lay sight on your form
you seem to wish the absence was a
lifetime.
We sit in silence both in our individual
zones
I wait patiently for you to send the
green light
allow me into your world and get
entangled in ourselves
but instead I toss and turn through
silent nights.

Dead eyes pay lip service to the salty
trails left behind.
The obligatory concern is strained,
lacking the emotional connect
immune to my sadness you remain stone
cold
but the warmth we once had I refuse to
forget.
I remain in my truth never wavering in
my faith
that little by little, one day you'll
meet me in the middle
your smile will return and beam in my
reflection
your eyes will be alive as our love
prepares for resurrection.

I remember the two hours per night we
conversated
the times you would come around when I
was feeling down or frustrated
the moments when you would make me feel
so elated
what we shared was a connection
underrated.
A connection that matured and advanced
too fast
a bond that quickly helped in making me
forget the past
our own world, our bubble, full of
happiness and laughs
something that can only be described as
a trance.

And I was there for you
The cheerleader to your life, the
groupie on the sides
your guiding light shining bright
an unbeatable might giving you a reason
to rise
I put my heart on the line because I was
your wife in disguise.

I remember those breathless nights we
created
the toe curling, yearning, emotion
stirring nights we debated
who would take control as our bodies
were invaded

with passion so deep we were more than
just naked.
More than just two people who became
entwined
surpassing lovers with just lust on
their minds
we weren't friends who had simply
stepped over the line
but entities captured by their matching
signs.

And I trusted you
When you cast me aside I swallowed my
pride
went along with your lies hoping all you
needed was time
then you'd go back to being mine so I
refused to cry
and I waited.. and waited for our stars
to align.

I remember the instant when it all
became clear
the light bulb flashed on and the hope
disappeared
I saw the ploy to keep me there, keep me
near
but never to admit, commit or show that
you cared.
Never to acknowledge or say I would
become your reject
but if you told me back then I would
never have believed it

we had the same dream and together we
could have achieved it
what we had was rare but maybe you
didn't need it.

But I loved you
My soul's disturbed what did I do to
deserve it?
the pain bleeds, it hurts how do I
reverse it?
I gave you my all and though I was far
from perfect
I know what we had and I know it was worth
it.

WISHES

I wish I could press rewind then replay
this entire soundtrack
I'd teach you to be resilient and not to
get so attached
to the trivial things that don't really
matter once you take a step back
and realise the bigger prize.
Yes, you are justified in your emotions
but sometimes it pays to ride with the
motion
and not get caught up with all these
notions
that you can't quite grasp or hold.

I wish I could fast forward and skip
through these challenging times
that have you struggling to remind
yourself that no matter how hard you
grind
things may not work out in your favour.
The strength of your labour doesn't
match the returns
even though you yearn
to have more. You soon learn
that life can't always be controlled.

I wish I could press pause to read the
entire break clause
take note of the terms and conditions
before embarking on this path of living.
The struggle of inequality that happens
generally
in genders but racially we're still
fighting to be free.
I believe in myself but who is it that
actually sees me?

I wish I could just stop instead of
learning on the job
so that I'd have time to right my wrongs
or find a better way to respond to the
home truths I've blocked.
Opportunities I could have realised if I
wasn't trying so hard to protect my
pride
These are not regrets but simple wonders
of a past life.

LOVERS ROCK

Love is blind but even through your
lying I can see the truth.
Though in denial I need to find the
damning proof.
The curse breeds in me, I know I could
leave but there's no use.
Don't want to be alone and do it on my
own, you're forcing me to choose
to be your concubine, you're no longer
mine. What's my excuse?
I used to be your wife and now I'm just
your prize used and abused.
Pressure dwells on my skin throbbing
from within, an everlasting bruise.
I'm watching ticking time and living off
your dime, you've got me in a noose.
As your future grows the more your anger
shows, you took my youth
over and over again no strength to
defend what is mine too.
If this survives it will never be
alright. Still, maybe it can soothe
the fire in your eyes when the hell is
alive deep inside you.
Tempers continue to rise as we both
reprise a false existing truce,
Yet we know from the past it will never
last as the sins accrue.
Addicted to you but can't take much more
you have me chopped and screwed,
because when deliverance comes, I'm
betting on my son that love will be
renewed.

The animosity plagues like a bacteria
taking over.
Not obligated to stay but too stubborn
to leave and so,
the fungus continues to grow.
Regular debates on the owner of fault,
the onus is sought
but neither will concede.
The greed to score another win
provides the only logic to be followed,
so emotions hollow from opposite sides
of the room.
Then meeting in the middle to fiddle
with versions of the truth
which only serve to continue this bitter
dispute.
The hostility is infectious
affecting everything we say and do,
leading to the breeding of infested
feelings
I loathe everything, don't believe
anything he says he'll do.
The virus turns stalemate,
I open my mouth but my voice makes him
cringe,
his eyes refuse mine like the sight of
me makes him sick.
Privately scheming and barely speaking
as this continues to decompose
the stench of contempt is rife,
it fills the air. It fills my nose.
I'm in mourning every morning realising
it's over for sure
but every night I fall asleep in hope
that tomorrow we'll find a cure.

STAINED

Her light can be found in many places
If you search hard enough you'll find the
traces
Scattered and painted in every shard
Shattered and discarded like broken glass
She finds a way to rebuild the picture
Keeps standing strong like a permanent
fixture
Stained but reframed and strong in her
stance
An alluring pane if you dare take a
glance.

Remember the ones that hurt you
The ones that befriended then burnt you
You serve them but they only swerve you
Those are the ones that'll learn you

Remember the ones that perverted you
Took for granted and didn't return it to
you
They succeeded when they coerced you
Those are the ones that cursed you

Favour the ones that alerted you
To the change and to the revert in you
They praise but are also stern with you
Those are the ones that concern you

Savour the ones that immerse you
In love, they never desert you
Those are the ones you can turn to
Those are the ones that deserve you.

PART THREE:

Then comes growth

IT'S MY PARTY

If I wasn't so preoccupied
trying to live someone else's life
maybe I wouldn't have been
this late to my own party
I got there in the end, it's true
but I'll cry if I want to
frustrated that I'm still waiting
for you to turn up and approve.

Your odd socks balled up and discarded
on the floor remind me of your bad
habits which I don't want to face
anymore.
Not lost but alone they stay, unclaimed
and unwanted. Stepped over and trodden
on, waiting to be acknowledged.

Your odd socks balled up and unwashed on
the floor remind me of your bad habits
which I'm not picking up anymore.
Unattached to good intentions and taking
up space, they've drifted away from
their partner but remain unfazed.

Your odd socks balled up and hidden
under the rug remind me of the bad
habits which you should have given up.
Too lazy to see and unwilling to try,
they get forgotten about and pushed
to the side.

Your odd socks balled up and brushed
under the carpet remind me of your bad
habits and why our lives parted.
A constant chore to keep them together,
now in hindsight it seems that not all
pairings are meant to last forever.

THE CROSSROADS

I couldn't go up, because I was down
and I felt the walls caving in around
I went into myself as I struggled to
breathe
alone with people but no one to
intervene.

It wasn't right, so I upped and went
left
my pace quickened with every step.
I needed to escape, to break out and be
free
I ran away from love because it ran away
from me.

I had hit rock bottom and it was a hard
from the top
because each way I turned, the path was
blocked
but I soldiered through life so I could
rise again.
It's a constant war when it's your
honour to defend.

When you've decided to move forward,
there's no turning back
you do what you can to keep yourself on
track.
break away from the naysayers and listen
to your mind
silence the noise and peace you will
find.

54

I smile when the sun rays rain down and
kiss my skin.
They burn a little and warm me from the
outside in, giving more richness to my
melanin.
And I soften.
I smile because I was born to be kissed
but I don't get it very often
so I lap it up when I can and pander to
its every sensation
in the hope it's never forgotten.

I stare at the ocean when it's an
endless sea of calm.
Soft silk caresses my skin and can do no
harm.
I stare with no judgement when she
decides to storm.
There's a rhythm to her madness and
reasons why she transforms
but if you don't delve beyond the
surface,
you'll never find her shore.

YOU DON'T KNOW

You don't know me anymore
But I haven't changed through the days
I've remained the same
the essence of me sticks like a stain.

You don't know me anymore
Refusing to see who stands before you
blemished and flawed
but has always been true.

You don't know me anymore
Line of sight blocked by void times
taking over your mind
and preventing us from getting it right.

You don't know me anymore,
And that hurts so much more
Than the insignificant reason you forgot
me for.

PIECES OF MY HEART

Her heart lay broken again.
Pieces scattered like dust stinging her
eyes
whilst she mourned loves newest
fatality.

Her body couldn't move.
Weighed down by sorrow, stubbornness
claimed her mind
as she clung onto a hopeless mentality.

Light was denied entry.
Consumed by the darkness the endless
days engulfed her
and she released all cares and vanity.

Alone she stayed.
Blocked out the world and indulged in
her decline
into self-inflicted insanity

Her heart lay mended again.
Significantly smaller than it used to
be
but beating profusely
fresh wounds stapled and stitched.

Each chapter had torn at it.
Passers-by had stolen chunks as
they crept in and out
taking what they wanted when they left.

Some gave their own which she eagerly
accepted.
Most trampled on it. Still.
The old scars were barely visible
and as she healed she closed the doors.

This time she decided to be selfish and
save a piece for herself.

He told me I looked beautiful and in my
head I replied -
Obviously. Obviously I look beautiful,
yes.
Because I have spent the whole day
avoiding carbs like the plague
so my stomach wouldn't bulge too far out
of my tight dress.
I'm so glad you noticed.
Because hours before I started the
'getting beautiful' process
I prepped my hair in twists so they
could set and look like this.
Beautiful. My stained puckered lips
curled up at the sides.
I'm smiling because you think my makeup
looks nice
not knowing the dark spots and
blemishes my foundation hides.
Will I still be beautiful walking around
in my socks and draws,
My old t-shirt and my uncovered flaws?
Satin bonnet or head scarf covering my
doo doo plaits
will you look at that with lustful eyes
and imagine the pleasures that I hold
inside?

When I've just washed my naps and they
shrink down to a level two, will my
teeny weeny afro still excite you?
We've never met so how would you know
what kind of beauty my self bestows?

I opened my mouth and replied "thank
you".
Because I'm not only beautiful... but
I'm polite too.

THIS BOY

Mama there's this boy
and I think that I love him.
He makes me feel secure
ain't no other that's like him.
I want to be with him night and day,
don't know why I'm even feeling this way.
Need time to heal from life
but what's life without him?

UNREQUITED

When your love for someone is not
returned
there's a sadness inside that slowly
burns
you try to suppress it and dismiss
the hurt
but there's no solace so in silence you
yearn.

For that day when their feelings will
change
all is mutual and your status is
claimed
relationship is natural, nothing forced
or strained
there's no longer any doubt that your
love will remain.

Until that day she is patient and she is
kind
accepts what she has and keeps him on
her mind
unconditional is her love so she
protects their time
it may not be perfect, for that is hard
to find.

She continues to play wife while he
leads her astray
anger boils inside sometimes but she'll
never say
guilt takes over so for forgiveness she
prays
her unrequited love will one day turn to
hate.

BATTLEFIELD

Ice has the power to tame the flame.
Fire has the strength to thaw the frozen.
Ice can't handle the heat and likes to
leave.
Fire will fight to warm the cold
shoulder.

I'm paining from the frustration of my
commitment being unreciprocated and
unappreciated.
No matter the levels of effort that I
gave it, it was wasted.
If only I had taken time and waited,
perhaps I would have been more receptive
to the mistake I was making and seen the
fake written all over you.

I confront and your tongue is tied,
tangled by the lies that your mouth
sings into my ears,
paying lip service to my fears, selling
the dream that I want to hear.
Unbeknownst that you're making promises
that won't ever be achieved, I'm being
deceived every time you speak and I'm
ashamed that it took me so long to see
it.

UGLY THINGS (REPRISE)

Ugly things can happen to beautiful
people
It doesn't mind nor matter if she wants
it or not
Keep giving her exactly what she hasn't
asked for
Don't listen when she silently screams
stop.
Wipe away her snot with your sleeve
Awkwardly smile when your eyes meet
Fill her head with sweet lyrics and take
what isn't yours
Discard her tarnished body now you've
removed what was once pure.

MY FLAWS

My flaws are roadmaps that lead me to
recollect your creation.
The sins of lovers harmonised into an
innocent combination.
You're my salvation.
A simple look in your eyes redeems any
hurt
I've found a true love that I never need
to return.

My flaws are stripes that I earned
whilst basking in your perfection.
This union will never be lost with your
light offering the direction.
You're a reflection.
In you I see what I am striving to
achieve
you give me strength because you are the
best of me.

STAR GAZER

I am at peace amongst the stars
They keep me focused, keep me calm
I question if that's where I'm supposed
to be
With them I feel safe, I feel homely.

I see all that they once were
They understand with no lines blurred
Do you wonder why my eyes often glisten?
I'm the child of stars. They hear, they
listen.

I'm a dream chaser living proud
A star gazer, head high in the clouds
You won't keep me low, try as you might
For the darkest of nights have stars so
bright.

THE LAST SONG

A song is not a secret to be kept.
but a lyric to be sung,
a melody to be hummed,
a beat to be drummed.

You wonder why I so often wept
the void space echoed,
with your voice in falsetto,
weak harmonies bellowed.

Whilst you silently crept
the record remained unmended,
it wasn't what I intended
when the song eventually ended.

www.ingramcontent.com/pod-product-compliance
Lightning Source LLC
Chambersburg PA
CBHW021938170626
46807CB00007B/3169